Where Is Max?

By Mary E. Pearson
Illustrated by Samantha L. Walker

Children's Press®
A Division of Grolier Publishing
New York • London • Hong Kong • Sydney
Danbury, Connecticut

To Duke, Dashley, Flower, Buddy, and Sweetpea
and the crazy searches you've sent me on!
—M. E. P.

For Jonathan
—S. L. W.

Reading Consultants
Linda Cornwell
Coordinator of School Quality and Professional Improvement
(Indiana State Teachers Association)

Katharine A. Kane
Education Consultant
(Retired, San Diego County Office of Education
and San Diego State University)

Library of Congress Cataloging-in-Publication Data
Pearson, Mary (Mary E.)
    Where is Max? / by Mary E. Pearson ; illustrated by Samantha L. Walker.
        p. cm. — (Rookie reader)
    Summary: When the class gerbil escapes from his cage, the children look
everywhere for it and find a way to get it to return home.
    ISBN 0-516-22019-5 (lib. bdg.)   0-516-27077-X (pbk.)
    [1. Gerbils—Fiction. 2. Schools—Fiction.] I. Walker, Samantha, ill. II. Title.
III. Series.
PZ7.P32316 Wh 2000
[E]—dc21   99-057172

Help! Where is Max?

3

We look inside.
We look outside.

We look up.
We look down.

Where is Max?

We look far.
We look near.

We look high.
We look low.

13

"Max! Max!" we call loudly.
"Max! Max!" we call softly.

Where is Max?

Hmm, Max's dish is empty.

But now it is full.

Max was lost, but now he is found!

Word List (29 words)

but	high	Max's
call	hmm	near
dish	inside	now
down	is	outside
empty	it	softly
far	look	up
found	lost	was
full	loudly	we
he	low	where
help	Max	

About the Author

Mary Pearson is a writer, teacher, mother, wife, chief-bottle-washer, and, of course, animal lover in San Diego, California. She has had a few wayward "Max's" in her life, but luckily, she has always outsmarted and found them—so far!

About the Illustrator

Since Samantha Walker was a little girl, she always carried a drawing instrument in her hand, whether she was running down the hall dragging an orange crayon along the wall, or doodling on the sidewalks with tanbark. She

has now graduated to other mediums, such as watercolor and ink, which she used to make the pictures for this book. Samantha has illustrated for various children's magazines, and this is her first book. Samantha lives in Colorado Springs, Colorado, with her husband, Jonathan, and their crazy cat, Tommy. Sometimes Tommy likes to play hide-and-seek, just like Max.